W9-APB-596

Sing-Along Holiday Stories

THE WORLD'S BIGGEST BIRTHDAY CAKE

By Carol Greene

Illustrations by Tom Dunnington

CHILDRENS PRESS®
CHICAGO

Library of Congress Cataloging in Publication Data

Greene, Carol.
The world's biggest birthday cake.

(Sing-along holiday stories)
Summary: Describes the making of the world's largest birthday cake to the tune of the American folk song "On Top of Old Smokey." Includes music.
1. Children's songs—United States. [1. Birthdays—Songs and music. 2. Cake—Songs and music. 3. Songs] I. Title.
PZ8.3.G82Wo 1985 784.5'05 85-16664
ISBN 0-516-08233-7 AACR2

Printed in the United States of America.
2 3 4 5 6 7 8 9 10 R 94 93 92 91 90

Because it's your birthday,
We wanted to make
You something quite special:
The world's biggest cake.

To haul in the flour
We rented a train.

The sugar came straight from
Hawaii by plane.

The eggs were a problem.
It took twenty hens.
They each laid a dozen,
Then started again.

We used someone's bathtub
To mix up the stuff,

Then twenty-four more, but
They still weren't enough.

1 2 3 4
19
20 21 22 23 24 25 26
27 28

For two weeks we baked it.
The smell was divine.
The timer went off on
Last Friday at nine.

We cooled it and iced it
With chocolate, of course,

Then brought it back home with
Ten mules and a horse.

We wanted some flowers
To put 'round the edge,
But they were too small, so
We planted a hedge.

The hedge needed water,
So we dug a lake,
And filled it with goldfish,
Ten frogs and a drake.

The lake was so pretty,
We put in a zoo,

Then added a circus,
A baseball game too.

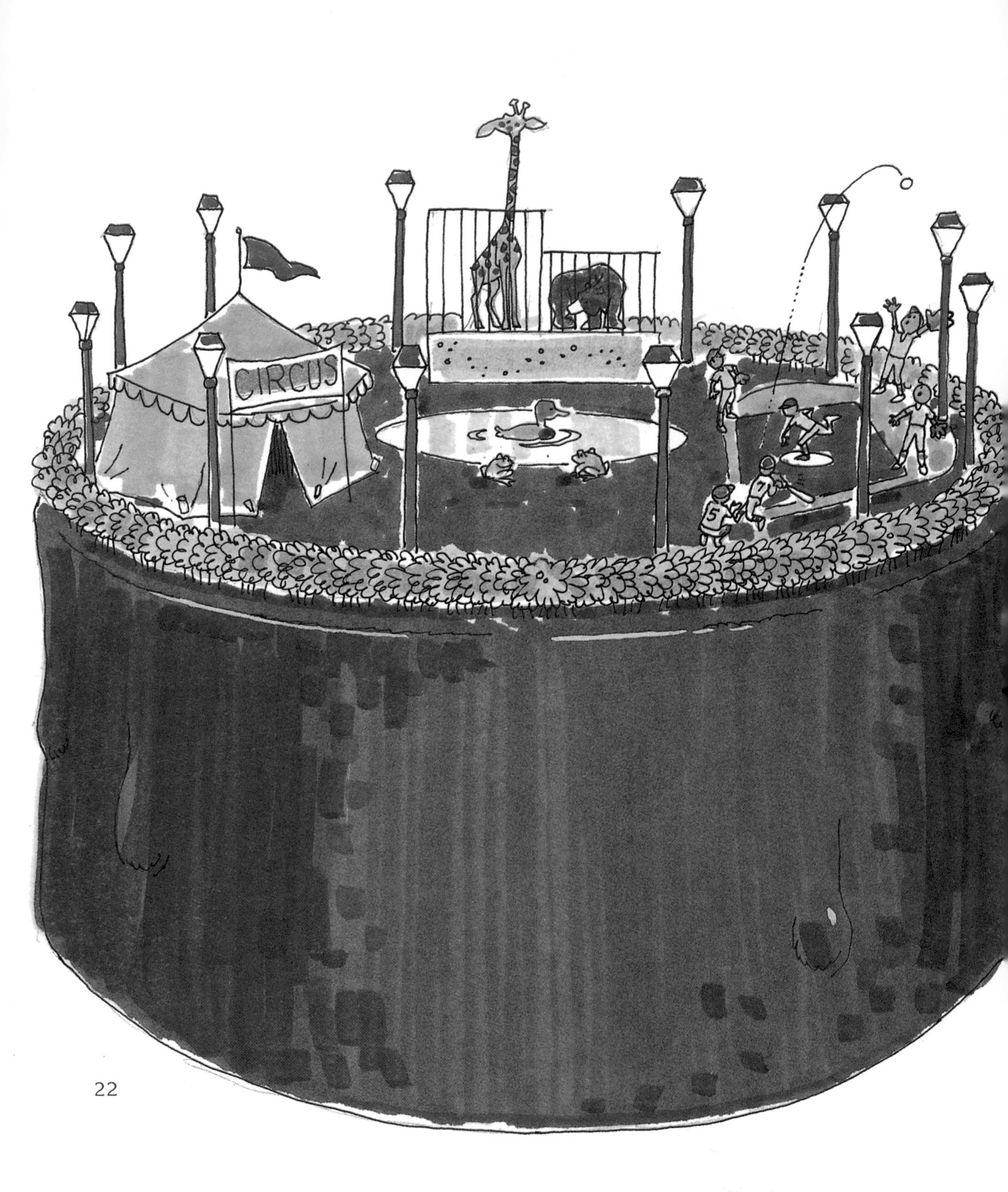
CIRCUS
5
7

With streetlights for candles,
It looked rather grand,
But just for good measure,
We hired a brass band.

At last all was ready.
The moment had come,
And we were so hungry,
We ate every crumb.

And now if you're tired of
These dumb birthday wishes,
Please do us a favor
And wash up the dishes.

Oh, by the way . . .

HAPPY BIRTHDAY!

HAPPY BIRTHDAY
KATIE

The World's Biggest Birthday Cake

5. The batter just fit in
   An old water tower.
   We found a volcano
   And turned on the power.

6. For two weeks we baked it.
   The smell was divine.
   The timer went off on
   Last Friday at nine.

7. We cooled it and iced it
With chocolate, of course,
Then brought it back home with
Ten mules and a horse.

8. We wanted some flowers
To put 'round the edge,
But they were too small, so
We planted a hedge.

9. The hedge needed water,
So we dug a lake,
And filled it with goldfish,
Ten frogs and a drake.

10. The lake was so pretty,
We put in a zoo,
Then added a circus,
A baseball game too.

11. With streetlights for candles,
It looked rather grand,
But just for good measure,
We hired a brass band.

12. At last all was ready.
The moment had come,
And we were so hungry,
We ate every crumb.

13. And now if you're tired of
These dumb birthday wishes,
Please do us a favor
And wash up the dishes.

About the Author

Carol Greene has a B.A. in English Literature from Park College, Parkville, Missouri and an M.A. in Musicology from Indiana University, Bloomington. She has worked with international exchange programs, taught music and writing, and edited children's books. She now works as a free-lance writer in St. Louis, Missouri and has had published over 50 books for children and a few for adults. When she isn't writing, Ms. Greene likes to read, travel, sing, and do volunteer work at her church. Her other books for Childrens Press include: *The Super Snoops and the Missing Sleepers; Sandra Day O'Connor: First Woman on the Supreme Court; Rain! Rain!; Please, Wind?; Snow Joe;* and *The New True Book of Holidays Around the World.*

About the Artist

Tom Dunnington divides his time between book illustration and wildlife painting. He has done many books for Childrens Press, as well as working on textbooks, and is a regular contributor to *Highlights for Children.* Tom lives in Oak Park, Illinois.